THE MAN OF STEEL™

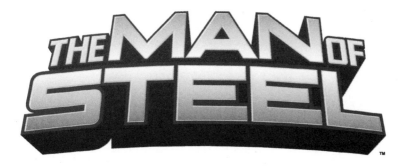

THE MAN OF STEEL

SUPERMAN AND THE MAN OF GOLD

WRITTEN BY
PAUL WEISSBURG

ILLUSTRATED BY
TIM LEVINS

SUPERMAN CREATED BY
JERRY SIEGEL AND
JOE SHUSTER

STONE ARCH BOOKS
a capstone imprint

PUBLISHED BY STONE ARCH BOOKS IN 2012
A CAPSTONE IMPRINT
1710 ROE CREST DRIVE
NORTH MANKATO, MN 56003
WWW.CAPSTONEPUB.COM

CATALOGING-IN-PUBLICATION DATA IS
AVAILABLE AT THE LIBRARY OF CONGRESS WEBSITE.

ISBN: 978-1-4342-4095-8 (LIBRARY BINDING)
ISBN: 978-1-4342-4222-8 (PAPERBACK)

SUMMARY: WHEN STOMPA AND THE DEMOLITION TEAM SEND
A MIGHTY EARTHQUAKE THROUGH METROPOLIS, ONLY ONE
MAN CAN SAVE THE CITY . . . BOOSTER GOLD! THE WORLD'S
NEWEST SUPER HERO KEEPS BEATING SUPERMAN TO
THE PUNCH. BUT SOON, THE MAN OF STEEL WONDERS IF
BOOSTER IS ALL GLITTER AND NO GOLD.

ART DIRECTOR: BOB LENTZ AND BRANN GARVEY
DESIGNER: HILARY WACHOLZ

PRINTED IN THE UNITED STATES OF AMERICA
IN STEVENS POINT, WISCONSIN.
112012   007056R

TABLE OF CONTENTS

Years ago in a distant galaxy, the planet Krypton exploded. Its only survivor was a baby named Kal·El who escaped in a rocket ship. After landing on Earth, he was adopted by the Kents, a kind couple who named him Clark. The boy soon discovered he had extraordinary abilities fueled by the yellow sun of Earth. He chose to use these powers to help others, and so he became Superman - the guardian of his new home.

He is...

THE MAN OF STEEL

™

CHAPTER 1

SURPRISE ATTACK

It was a beautiful day in Metropolis. The morning had begun with a brightly shining sun and fluffy white clouds scattered across the sky. Clark Kent was in an especially good mood because spring had finally arrived.

At noon, Clark met his coworkers and friends, Lois Lane and Jimmy Olsen, on the rooftop of the Daily Planet Building. Clark and Lois were both reporters for the *Daily Planet* newspaper, and Jimmy was a photographer.

Today, they were in charge of covering an annual hot air balloon race in the neighboring county. The high-rise rooftop gave them a great view of the event. And, since the weather was so pleasant, the trio decided to eat lunch up there as well.

Lois did not enjoy cooking, so she had brought a large ice-filled cooler to the roof.

"What's inside?" Jimmy asked.

"You'll see," Lois said with a smile.

Clark was tempted to use his X-ray vision to look inside the cooler and see what she'd brought, but he didn't want to ruin her surprise. So he waited patiently.

After they had all finished their lunches, Lois finally opened the cooler. Inside was a small carton of ice cream and three ice cream cones.

"That's it?" Jimmy asked, clearly disappointed. "What's so special about plain old ice cream?"

"Just try it," Lois told him. She carefully placed three scoops of ice cream onto each cone, and then she passed the cones to her friends.

Jimmy licked the melting scoop. His face broke into a huge smile. "It's Jurgens' ice cream!" he said. "How is that possible?"

Jurgens' Ice Cream Emporium was Metropolis's most popular ice cream shop. Lines to get ice cream during the hotter days wrapped around many city blocks. However, the shop was only open during the summer. "Last year," Lois explained, "I bought a carton of ice cream before Jurgens closed for the winter. I've been saving it ever since."

"I'm impressed you didn't eat it all yourself!" Jimmy joked. "I doubt I'd be able to resist, knowing it was in the freezer the whole time."

Lois and Clark laughed and shook their heads. As they all happily ate their ice cream, the day seemed like it was going to be a perfect.

But that's when a large, angry woman in body armor appeared in the middle of Metropolis. Her voice rang out across the entire city. "Out of my way!" she shouted. "I'm Stompa, and I'm gonna smash Metropolis to pieces!"

Lois, Clark, and Jimmy walked over to the edge of the roof and watched as Stompa marched down the busiest street in the city. A car got too close to her, so Stompa smashed her foot into its hood.

SMASSSSH! The car was shattered into a million pieces!

Using his X-ray vision, Clark saw that no one was badly hurt. It was only a matter of time, though, until someone was seriously injured. Stompa needed to be stopped.

"We'd better evacuate," Clark told his friends. "If Stompa reaches the Daily Planet Building, I don't want to be here to greet her."

"Relax," Lois told him. "Superman will show up. He'll take care of this lady before we've even finished our ice cream."

Of course, Lois didn't know that Clark Kent was actually Superman. Clark needed to get away from Lois and Jimmy so that he could change into his costume. Otherwise, no one would come to stop Stompa.

"Well, you can stay here if you want," Clark told them, pretending to be frightened. "But I'm getting out of here."

Lois and Jimmy watched as Clark raced down the stairs that led back inside the Daily Planet Building.

"Clark's a good guy," Lois told Jimmy, "but he sure is a coward!"

* * *

Seconds later, Superman flew past the Daily Planet Building. He landed directly in front of Stompa.

"What's this all about?" Superman asked.

Stompa smashed both her feet into the ground. *RUMMMMMMMMMMMBLE!* A shock wave rushed at the Man of Steel. *CRUNCH!*

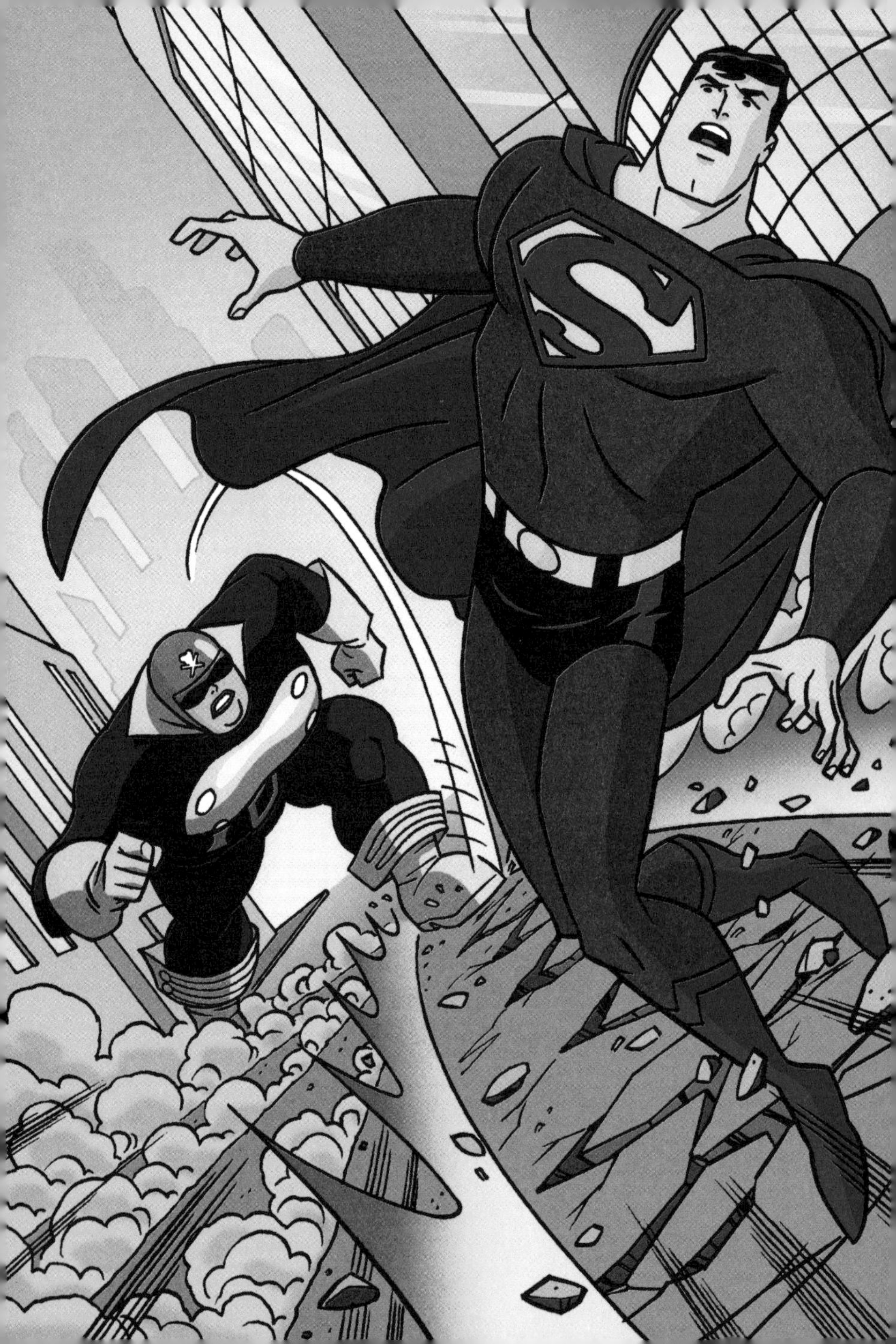

Superman was thrown back by the powerful blast. He crashed into the wall of a nearby restaurant with a *THUD!*

"Ha! I just knocked out Superman!" Stompa shouted. "Let's see what the Guide says about that!"

Atop the Daily Planet Building, Jimmy was taking pictures of the fight. After all, he was a photographer — and someone knocking out Superman was big news.

Turning to Lois, Jimmy asked, "Who — or what — is the Guide?"

"I don't know," Lois told him. "But I have a feeling we'd better find out."

Superman slowly crawled to his knees. His whole body ached, but it'd take a whole lot more than that to keep the Man of Steel from protecting his adopted home.

Stompa saw that Superman was trying to stand. "Why are you even bothering to get up?" Stompa asked. "I'm just gonna knock you back down again!"

"Looks like Superman could use a little help," Lois said. She looked at the food they'd been eating just moments ago. Lois picked up her cooler of ice cream and carried it to the side of the roof.

"Hey, Stompa!" Lois called out loudly. "It's lunch time!" Then she dropped the cooler over the edge of the building.

"Lois, no!" Jimmy cried out in horror. "The ice cream!"

The cooler plummeted toward Stompa. The super-villain turned around and looked up to see who had called her name. Just then, a cooler full of ice cream struck her square in the face!

SPLAAAAT!

"You're gonna pay for that!" Stompa shouted. "No one messes with Stompa!"

"Maybe we should back away from the edge of the roof," Jimmy suggested.

"Don't worry," Lois told him. "Stompa is hundreds of feet below us. How's she going to reach us from there?"

Stompa bent her knees and jumped two feet into the air. As she landed, she slammed both her boots into the ground. **SMAAASSSSSSH!** The force from the blast rippled along the street, then headed up the side of the Daily Planet Building.

RUMMMMMMMMMMBLE!

The entire building shook with violent force.

Jimmy barely managed to hang on to the side of the roof, but Lois — along with her half-eaten ice cream cone — was thrown off the edge.

"Superman!" Lois cried out.

The Man of Steel looked up to see Lois plummeting toward the ground. The hero tried desperately to get up, but he couldn't. His body was still too shaken from Stompa's massive attack.

At that moment, a man in a bright blue-and-gold uniform came swooping down out of the sky.

The hero paused in midair, struck a pose, and shouted, "Never fear, Booster Gold is here!"

A golden metal robot, no bigger than a football, flew by his side.

An electronic voice came from the robot's speaker. "You may want to hold off on the introductions, sir," it said. "I think that young lady is about to hit the ground."

"Quiet, Skeets," Booster replied. "You're ruining my big entrance."

WOOOOOOOOOSH! Booster Gold flew toward Lois Lane. He caught her in his powerful arms.

"Congratulations," the man told her. "You've just been saved by Metropolis's newest and greatest and most handsome super hero . . . Booster Gold!"

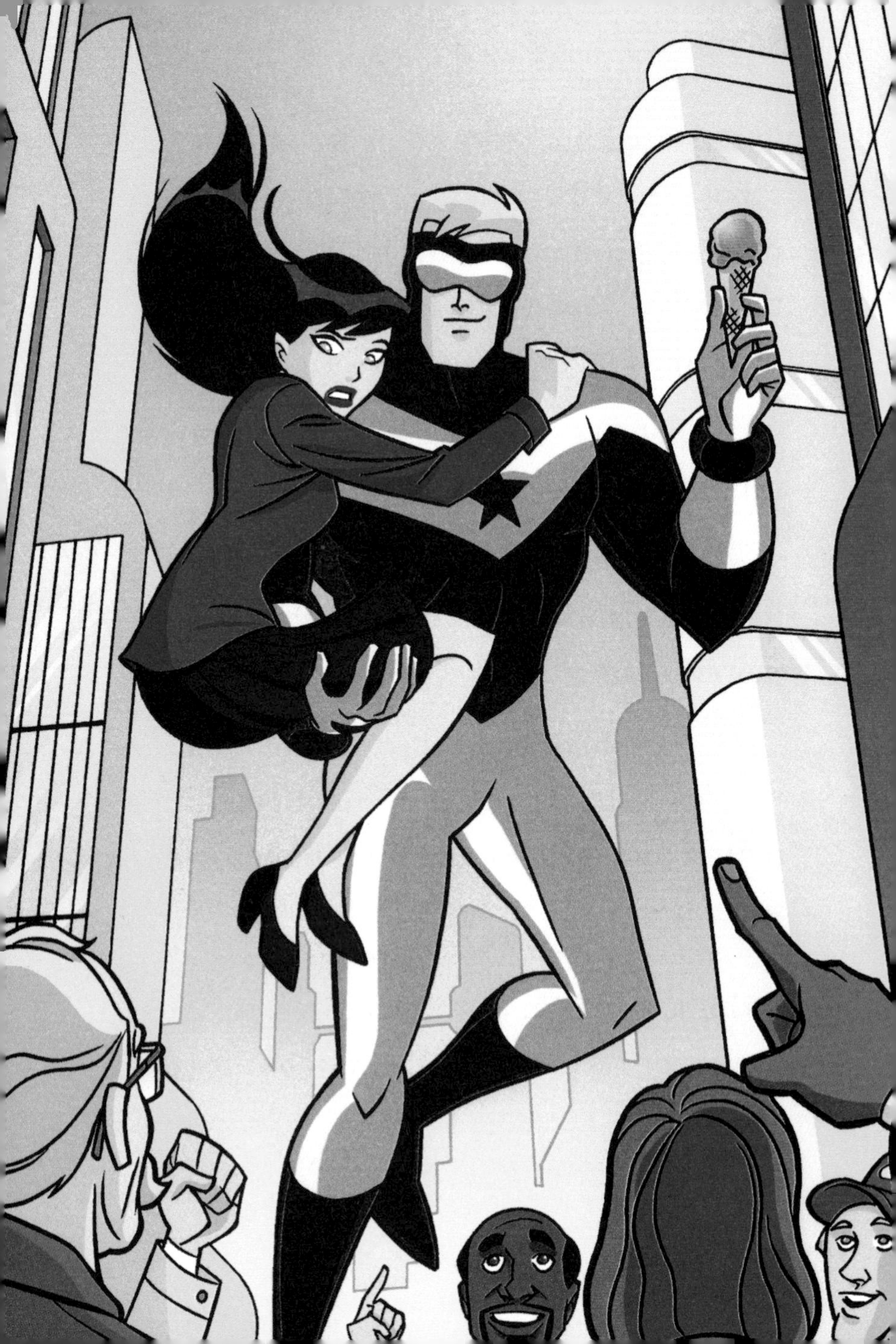

CHAPTER 2

BOOSTER WHO?

Booster Gold, still carrying Lois in his arms, swooped down. The new hero caught Lois's ice cream cone just before it splattered on the ground.

Lois began to speak, but Booster Gold cut her off. "There's no need to thank me," he told Lois as he placed her safely on the ground and handed her the ice cream. "The satisfaction that comes with saving innocent citizens is all the reward I need." Booster stood with his hands on his hips and a million-dollar smile on his face.

As Booster Gold posed for Lois, the Daily Planet Building continued to shake. Pieces of the building's exterior were beginning to fall off the building. Superman was so shocked he could barely stand, but he used his heat vision to blast apart the loose bricks before they could hit the ground.

RRRUMMMMMMMMMBLE!

There was a horrible, loud noise as a huge section of the building suddenly fell away from the foundation. Booster Gold seemed unaware that he, and several other people, were about to be crushed.

Thankfully, Superman had finally recovered enough to fly. He raced to the Daily Planet Building and grabbed ahold of the section that was breaking apart. He struggled to keep it from falling with his arms.

"Everyone, get out of the building!" Superman cried out. "I can't hold this up much longer!"

Inside the Daily Planet Building, everyone began to evacuate. They knew that if Superman let go, they would all be crushed.

Meanwhile, a group of photographers had gathered around Booster Gold.

SNAP! CLICK! SNAP! They took picture after picture as Booster Gold posed for them, holding his arms up triumphantly. "How do I look?" he asked them.

Lois frowned at Booster Gold. "If you're such a hero, shouldn't you be helping Superman?" she asked.

Booster glanced over at Superman. He was still struggling to hold up the building.

"He seems to be doing okay," Booster said, turning back at the cameras. "Besides, these people want to take my picture, and I hate to disappoint my fans!"

Booster turned to Skeets. "Psst, Skeets!" he whispered. "Don't forget the T-shirts."

Skeets opened a box of T-shirts. "Free T-Shirts! Get your Booster Gold T-Shirts!" he announced. "Not yet available in stores. They're great collector's items."

Booster put one arm around Lois Lane. "Hey, get a picture of us together," he told the photographers. "You can use this headline: 'Booster Gold saves Lois Lane!'"

Lois shoved him away. "Or they could call it, 'Booster Gold stands around posing for pictures while a falling building crushes citizens!'" she said.

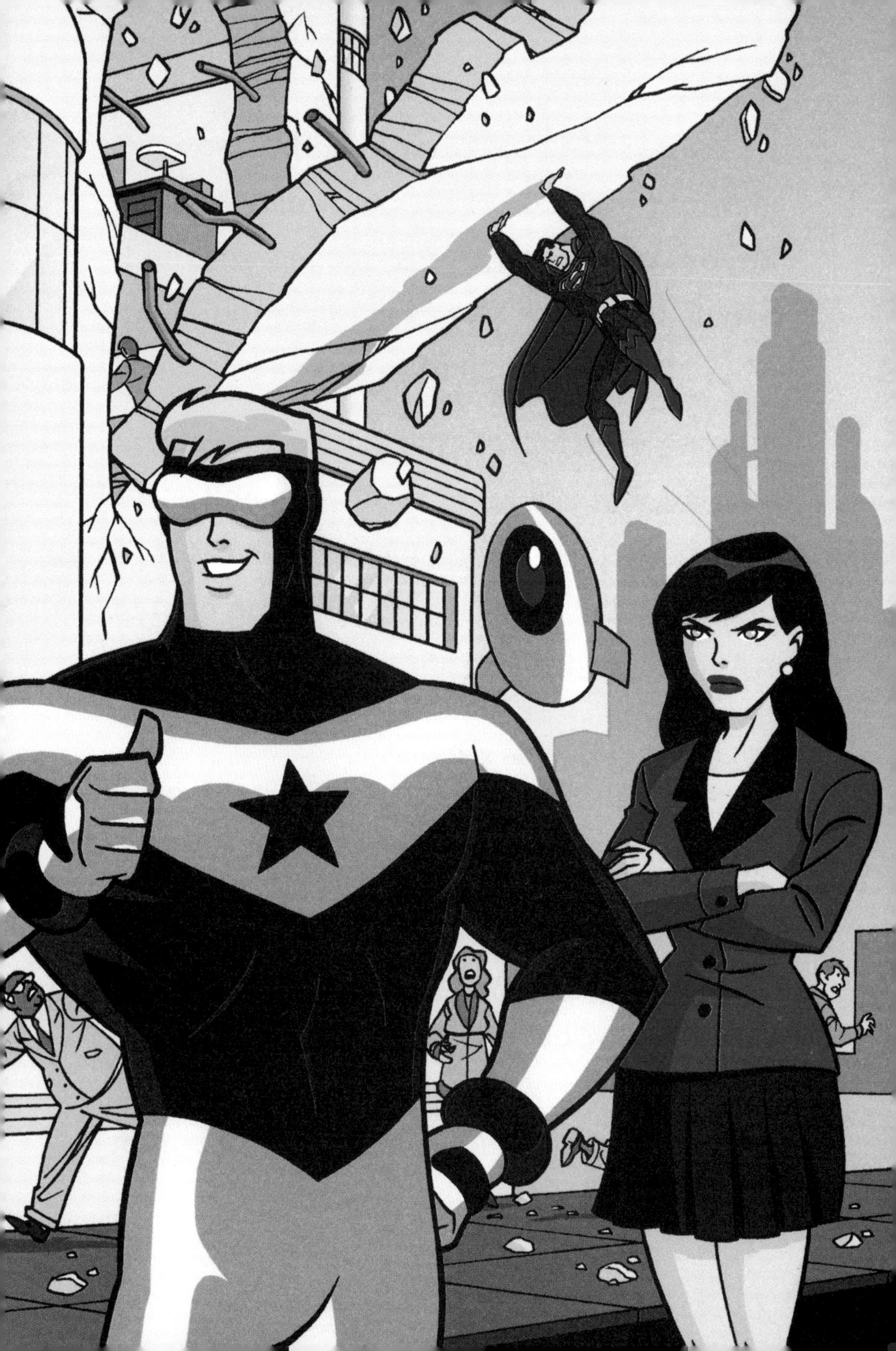

Meanwhile, Superman used his X-ray vision to make sure that the Daily Planet Building was empty. After the last few people had exited, he released the building. Chunks of rubble fell from its walls.

Superman looked and saw Lois arguing with Booster Gold and Skeets. A small crowd of reporters took pictures. The Man of Steel didn't know what was going on, but Lois appeared to be safe, and that was all that mattered.

Next, Superman searched for Stompa. The super-villain had disappeared. He couldn't find her anywhere.

Finally, Superman used his X-ray vision to see if anyone had been hurt by Stompa's attack. No one was seriously injured, but one man had a mild concussion. Superman carried him to the nearest hospital.

Meanwhile, Booster Gold was finishing his first public appearance. "I'd love to stay and let you take more pictures," Booster Gold told the crowd of reporters, "but I have to go. After all, a super hero's work is never done!"

"But you haven't told us anything about yourself," one reporter exclaimed.

"Where are you from? What are your superpowers?" another reporter asked.

Booster flashed a big grin at the reporters. "Don't worry," he told them. "You'll be seeing plenty more of me — and my powers — very soon!"

*　　*　　*

The next day, Lois, Clark, and Jimmy Olsen were inside what remained of the Daily Planet Building.

The headline of the newspaper read: BOOSTER GOLD SAVES THE DAY!

Lois suddenly threw that morning's newspaper onto the floor. "I hate Booster Gold!" she yelled.

Clark eyed the paper and frowned. Beneath the headline, in much smaller letters, the sub-headline read: SUPERMAN LENDS HELPING HAND. "Well," Clark said, "I guess Booster did save your life."

"And your ice cream cone," Jimmy said with a smirk.

Lois glared at both of them. "Yes," she said, "and then he spent the next half hour posing for pictures while Stompa escaped. Superman rescued everyone inside the Daily Planet Building!"

Lois took a deep breath.

"Anyway," Lois continued, "I've been doing a little research into that Guide Stompa mentioned yesterday."

"Did you figure out what she was talking about?" Clark asked.

"I think so," Lois said. "Look at this." She pointed to her computer screen at a website titled: A Guide to Super-villains.

"Oh, yeah, I've heard of this!" said Jimmy. "They do super-villain reviews."

"Super-villain reviews?" Clark asked.

"That's right," Jimmy told him. "They rate super-villains' costumes, their superpowers, if they have a cool name or an interesting gimmick. That sort of thing."

"They rank the super-villains?" Clark asked. He'd been fighting super-villains as Superman for many years.

Despite his extensive experience battling super-criminals, the idea of ranking his most formidable foes had never occurred to the super hero.

"Yep," said Lois, turning the laptop toward Clark. "See for yourself."

Clark looked at the list. He found Stompa toward the bottom. She was ranked number 483 out of 500. "Ouch!" said Clark. "No wonder Stompa was so angry. She barely even made the list."

"Well," Jimmy said, "you have to admit, her costume is pretty ugly."

Then Jimmy looked more closely at the list. "According to this, Stompa ranked between the Bug-Eyed Bandit and Ding Dong Daddy!"

Lois made a face. "Ding Dong Daddy?"

Jimmy grinned. "He's actually pretty cool — I mean, for a super-villain. I would have ranked him much higher."

Lois looked skeptical. "Jimmy, the man calls himself Ding Dong Daddy. How cool can he be?"

SLAM!

At that moment, the editor-in-chief of the *Daily Planet*, Perry White, stormed through the room's double doors. "Can someone tell me why my two of my best reporters are standing around?" he shouted. "A few blocks away, Stompa is attacking the mayor at City Hall!"

Lois's eyes went wide. "We're on our way, Chief!" she said, grabbing Jimmy's arm. They raced out the door, Jimmy tripping over his own feet.

Perry watched them leave with a frown on his face. "Why can't they be more punctual like you, Clark?" he said with a sigh. He turned to face his favorite reporter and saw that he had already left. "Clark?"

Clark had snuck inside an empty storage room during the commotion and changed into his uniform.

After all, this was a job for Superman!

*   *   *

It only took Superman a few seconds to fly to City Hall, but he was too late. Stompa had already left — and Booster Gold was standing next to the mayor of Metropolis as a crowd of photographers took their picture. "If it weren't for Booster Gold, Stompa might have destroyed City Hall — and me!" said the mayor.

"Booster Gold is a hero!" he exclaimed.

"It's just fortunate that I happened to be nearby," said Booster Gold.

Superman watched from a distance. He thought about what Lois had said earlier. It did seem like a pretty big coincidence that Booster Gold was around both times Stompa attacked. Was Lois right about Booster?

The mayor looked up and saw Superman. "You're too late, Superman!" the mayor cried out. "I'm just lucky that Metropolis has another super hero to protect us from evildoers!"

One of the reporters asked, "Does this mean that you're officially endorsing Booster Gold instead of Superman?"

"You bet it does!" the mayor replied.

"Booster Gold is the kind of hero this city needs," the mayor added. "And that's why a week from today will be a new holiday: Booster Gold Day! Everyone in Metropolis can come together and celebrate this city's greatest hero!"

Booster Gold beamed with pride.

As the reporters asked the mayor about the new holiday, Superman flew away. This was no time to pose for pictures. He needed to find Stompa and stop her before she caused even more harm.

The Man of Steel heard a voice call out. "Superman! Superman!" it said. "Can you hear me?"

Superman looked around.

Where is that voice coming from? wondered the Man of Steel.

Then Superman saw a strange figure on a nearby rooftop. It almost looked like a ghost.

As he flew closer, Superman could see that it was his old friend, Rip Hunter. Rip was a time traveler from the future. The reason that Rip Hunter looked like a ghost was because he wasn't really there at all. Superman was looking at a hologram that Rip Hunter used in order to avoid accidentally altering history.

Although Rip was not allowed to interfere directly in the 21st century, he sometimes helped Superman battle evil time travelers and super-villains from the future.

THUMP! Superman landed. "It's good to see you, Rip," the Man of Steel said. "Is everything okay?"

"I'm afraid not, Superman," Rip replied. "I'm here to warn you about a criminal who has traveled to your time from the 25th century!"

This was bad. Villains from the future had access to advanced technology to commit their crimes. That made them dangerous enemies, and they were always very difficult to capture.

"I don't think I've seen any super-villains from the future lately," Superman told his friend. "Can you describe him?"

"Oh, you've seen him, all right," Rip Hunter said. "His name is Booster Gold!"

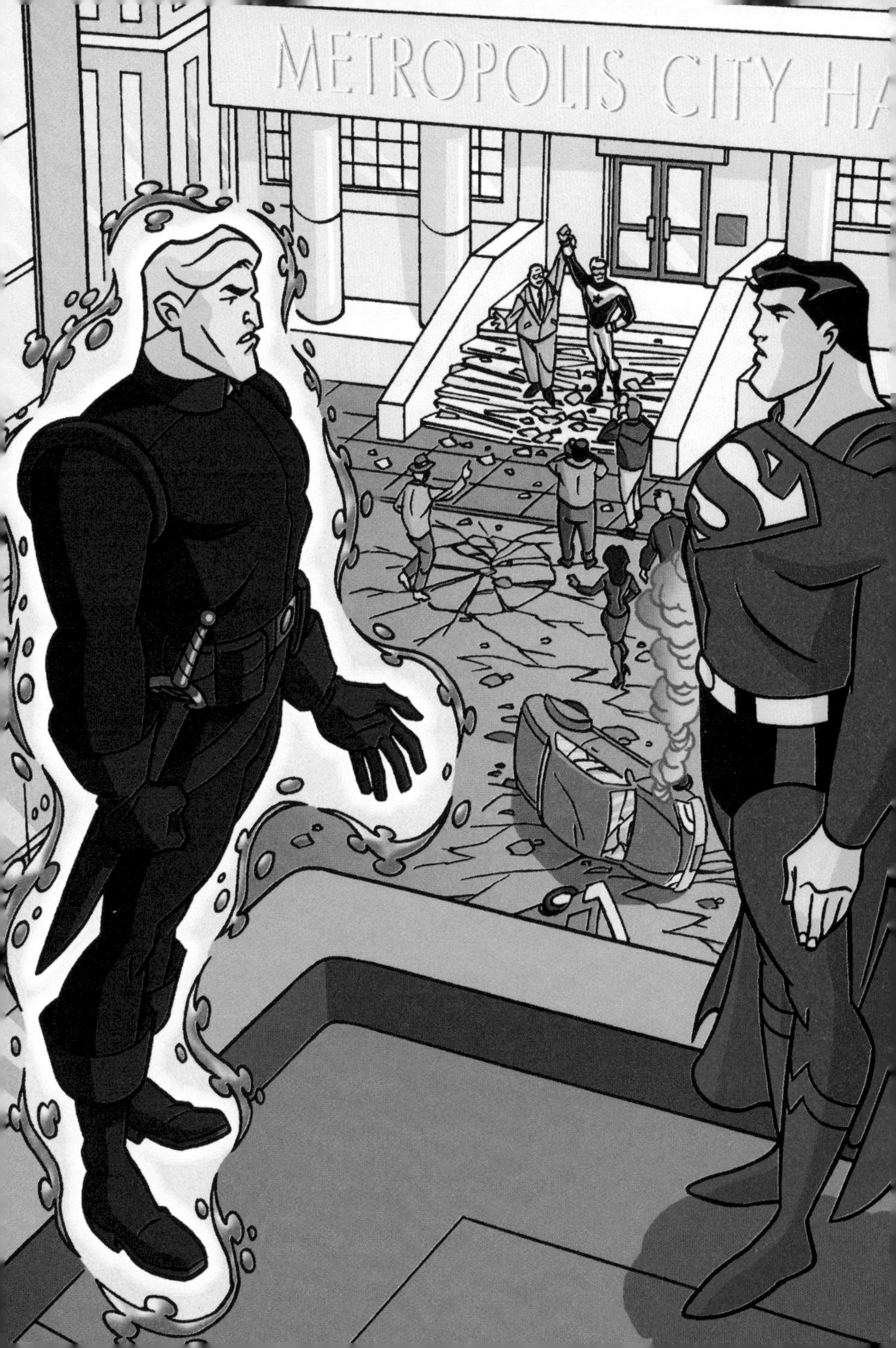
METROPOLIS CITY HA

CHAPTER 3

FUTURE CRIMES

"Booster Gold is a criminal from the future?" Superman asked. He couldn't believe it. Booster was pretty irresponsible at times, but he certainly didn't seem like a super-villain.

"It's true," Rip Hunter told him. "I brought this holo-video to show you."

A three-dimensional picture appeared before Superman. It was a hologram, just like Rip Hunter. It showed a young man inside a museum sweeping the floor. The museum was filled with futuristic machines.

"That's Michael Jon Carter," said Rip Hunter. "And this scene takes place in the 25th century — almost 400 years in your future!"

"That guy is Booster Gold?" Superman asked.

"Not yet," Rip told him. "Before he became Booster Gold, Michael worked as a janitor at the Metropolis Space Museum. It was a decent job, but that wasn't enough for him. He wanted glory. He wanted to be famous!"

Superman watched as the holo-video showed Michael Jon Carter's daily life. When Michael rode the Meta-Train to work, no one seemed to notice him. When Michael walked through the sky-tubes at night, no one smiled at him or said hello.

"He doesn't seem like such a bad guy," said the Man of Steel. "Just lonely."

The next picture showed Michael using his keys to sneak into the Metropolis Space Museum late at night. Superman watched as Michael took a Legion Flight Ring from a display case. Then he saw Michael steal a force-field belt from another section of the museum. Soon, Michael Jon Carter no longer looked like a janitor. Instead, he was dressed as Booster Gold!

The holo-video continued. Suddenly, a golden, football-sized robot entered the picture. It was the museum's security droid.

"Return those objects," Skeets ordered Booster Gold. "Otherwise, you will be arrested!"

"Not a chance," Booster told him.

"Here in the 25th century," Booster said, "I'm nobody. But I'm going to travel back to the 21st century and use this stuff to become the greatest hero who ever lived."

Booster Gold stepped into a time-travel machine and set the dial for the 21st century.

WOOOOOOOSH! Booster disappeared from sight!

Skeets paused, and then followed Booster into the machine.

ZIP! Skeets vanished too!

Superman watched as the holo-video showed Booster Gold and Skeets appearing in Metropolis in the 21st century. Skeets was still trying to capture Booster Gold, but then Booster stopped running.

"Hey," Booster said. "Why are you trying to arrest me?"

"You stole those weapons from the museum," Skeets told him.

Booster Gold paused. Then a smile crept across his face. "But that hasn't happened yet!" he said excitedly. "That crime happened in the 25th century. We're in the 21st century. That crime won't happen for another 400 years."

CRACKLE! CRACKLE! Skeets blinked and sparked. To Superman, it seemed like the robot was confused — if robots were capable of such a thing.

"Look, Skeets," Booster said, "We're in the 21st century, so let's enjoy ourselves. With your help, and your historical database, I could become the greatest hero that ever lived."

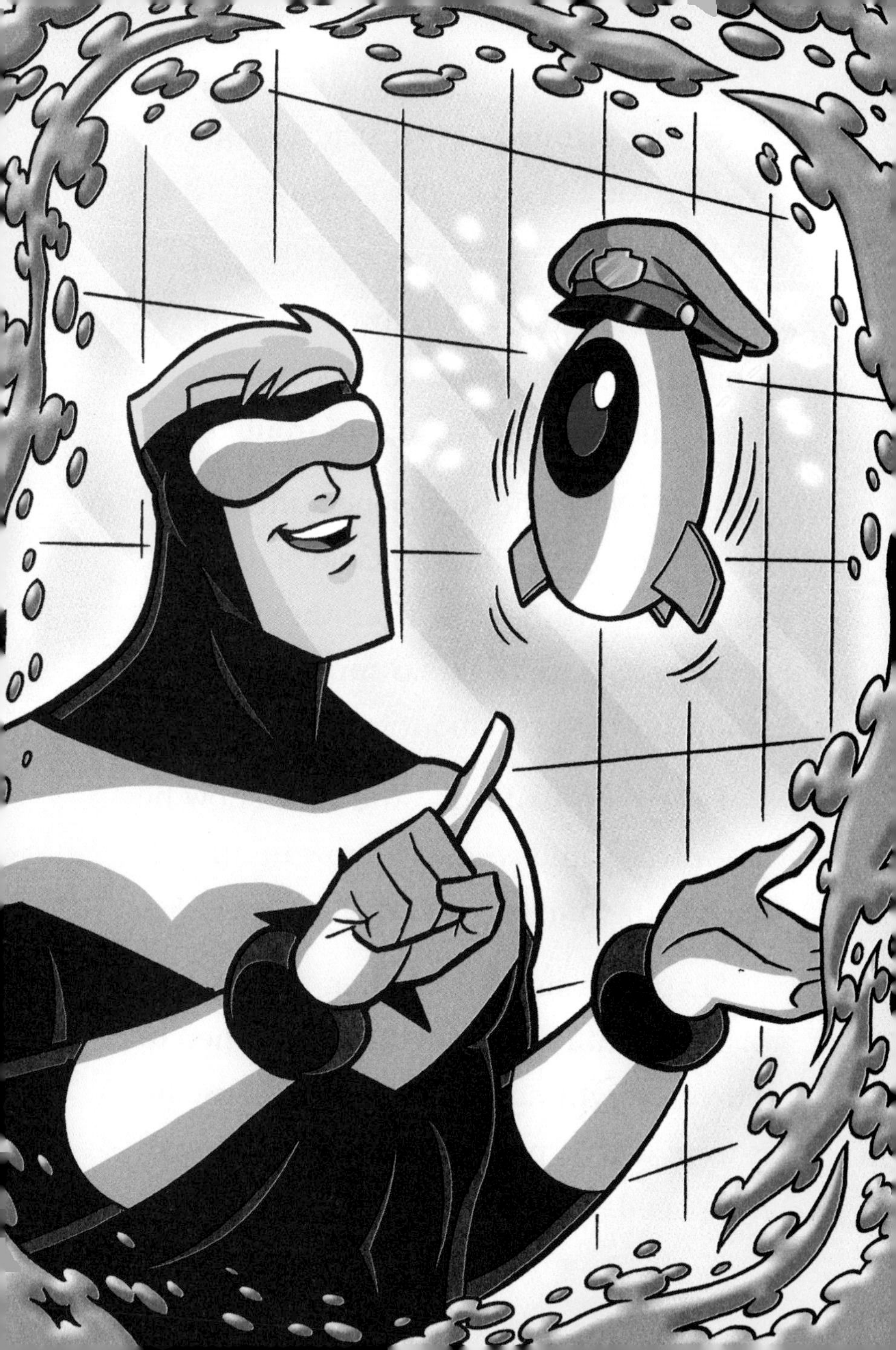

Booster grinned at the security bot. "Would you like to be my manager?" he asked.

The holo-video faded away. Despite himself, Superman smiled. Booster Gold sure could talk his way out of trouble.

"You know what happened after that," Rip Hunter said. "Booster Gold is using those weapons he stole from the future to make people think he's a super hero. But, really, all he cares about is being famous."

Superman nodded. "And that's how he knew when and where to show up in order to save the mayor," added the Man of Steel.

"Exactly," said Rip Hunter. "This is all history to him. He knows exactly when and where everything will happen because he is from a time period where it has already happened."

Rip's hologram looked Superman in the eyes. "And Booster Gold is using that information to appear at critical moments and pretend to be a hero!" said Rip.

"That would be bad enough," Superman said, "but he's also being very reckless. It's only a matter of time before his showboating gets someone seriously hurt. Or killed." Superman looked at Rip with determined eyes. "What do you need me to do?"

"Capture Booster Gold and Skeets and send them back to the 25th century where they belong," Rip explained. "If Booster Gold stays here, he might accidentally change his own history and create a time paradox." His voice became grim. "That would put the entire universe in danger, Superman."

"It's too bad," Superman said. "I think that deep down inside, Michael is a good person. He could have used those weapons to become a super-villain, but he chose to become a hero, instead."

"Don't be fooled," warned Rip Hunter. "Booster Gold is a criminal. He doesn't care about anyone or anything but himself."

Superman wasn't so sure about that, but he knew that he could trust Rip Hunter. And he was right about one thing: Booster Gold and Skeets had to be sent back to the 25th century . . . and fast.

*   *   *

Meanwhile, Stompa was holding a meeting in a local diner with a group of super-villains called the Demolition Team.

The Demolition Team had worked out of Coast City for a few years, where they'd fought Green Lantern on more than one occasion. The team was led by Rosie, who carried a rapid-fire hot riveter. The other members of the team were Hardhat, whose powered helmet and harness gave him super-strength, Jackhammer, whose weapon of choice was a giant jackhammer, Scoopshovel, whose hydraulic power-arm could dig through anything, and Steamroller, who drove an actual steamroller that he used to flatten anything that stood in his way!

Stompa was offering them some work. "It'll raise my super-villain ranking to have a team of super-villains working for me," Stompa explained. "And it will help your rankings to work for the villain who beat up Superman!"

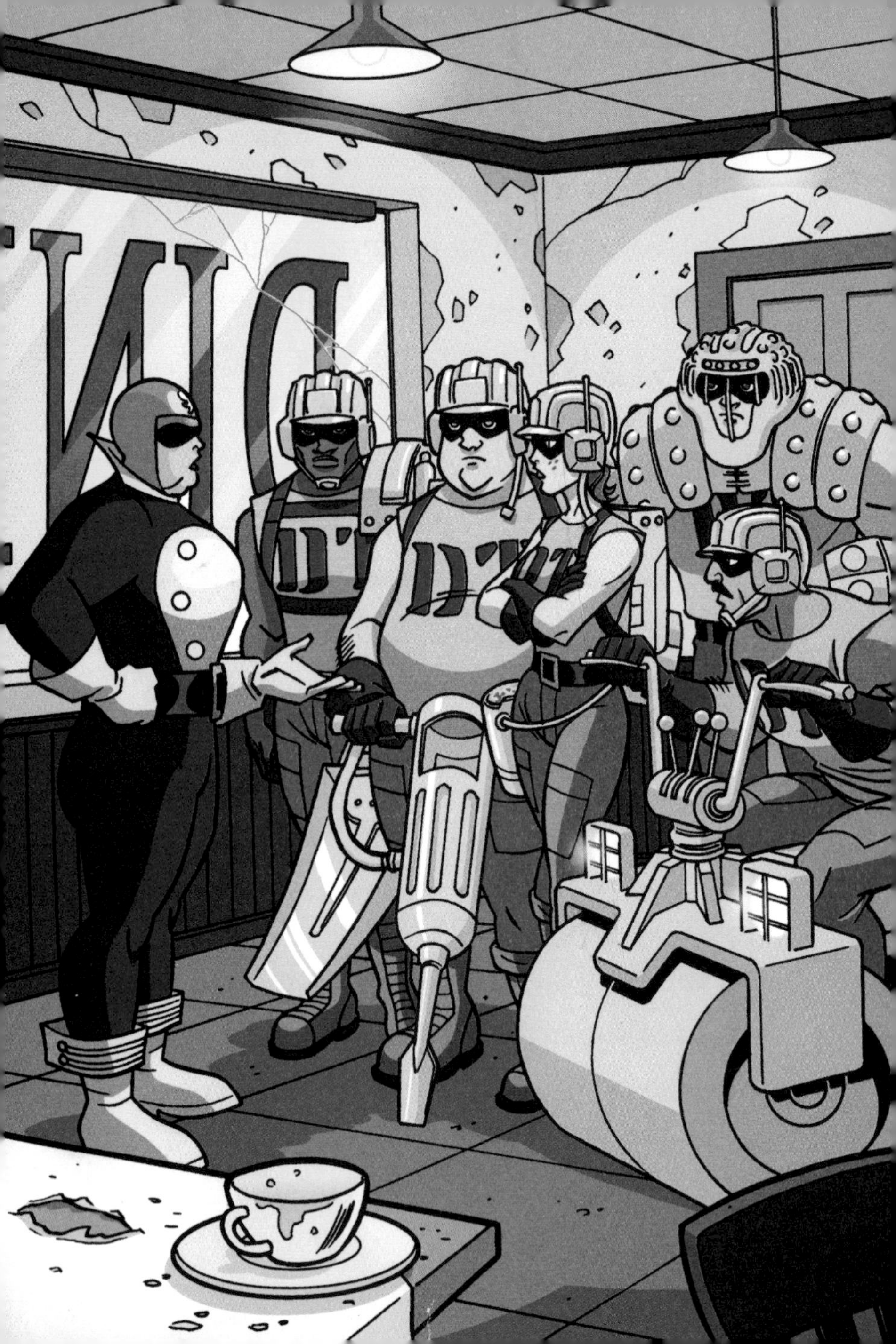

"I don't know," Rosie said. "You knocked Superman down, but one lucky strike doesn't make you the mother lode!"

"Are you serious?" Stompa said. "I could've killed Superman if it hadn't been for that blasted ice cream cooler."

"Prove it," Rosie told her.

"You want proof?" Stompa said. "Then you got it! I'm gonna show up at the Booster Gold Day celebration and destroy Metropolis . . . once and for all!"

CHAPTER 4

BOOSTER GOLD DAY

A week later, Booster was helping with the final preparations for the Booster Gold Parade.

"It sure is nice of you to help us like this," said the woman in charge of the day's events. She had workers setting up vending stands and closing off the streets for the big parade.

Booster was using his flight ring to hang the blue-and-gold banners. They read: METROPOLIS LOVES BOOSTER GOLD!! (AND SKEETS.)

"No problem," Booster said. "After all, it's for a good cause."

WOOOOOOSSH! Superman flew down to meet the new hero.

"Booster," the Man of Steel said, "I need to talk to you."

"Sure," said Booster with a big smile. "Let's talk."

Superman led Booster and Skeets to a nearby rooftop where no one would overhear their conversation. "I know who you are, Michael," said Superman. "And I know that you're from the 25th century."

Booster's smile quickly vanished. "I can explain —" he began to say.

"That isn't necessary," Superman told him. "But you need to return to the 25th century right away."

Superman frowned. "Every minute that you spend in the 21st century risks changing history," he said. "That's very dangerous — for everyone."

Booster gazed down at the people setting up for the Booster Gold Day Parade. There were hot dog stands and cotton candy vendors lining the streets. People were selling Booster Gold T-shirts, buttons, and balloons. There were even Booster Gold action figures.

And then there was the Booster Gold statue. It was hidden beneath a giant tarp, but Booster had sneaked a look earlier. The statue was gigantic! Everyone in Metropolis would be able to look up and see Booster's huge face smiling down at them.

Booster Gold really wanted to be there for the unveiling of the statue.

He'd already written his speech. It wasn't fair that he would have to miss all the fun.

Booster Gold smiled again. "You're right, Superman," he finally said. "It's time for me to go back and pay for my future crimes."

"I'm glad you're being reasonable about this," said Superman. "I was afraid you might try to escape."

"No," said Booster. "I'm ready to accept the consequences of my actions. But, before I go, there is one thing I need to tell you." Booster Gold looked around, as if making sure that no one else was listening to their conversation. "There's a secret reason I came back here to the 21st century — and it wasn't just to become a super hero!"

Superman narrowed his eyes. "It wasn't?" he asked.

"I came to warn you about a horrible disaster," Booster explained. "There's a meteor shower headed straight for Earth right now. If you don't stop it, the results will be catastrophic!" Booster Gold pulled out a small, electronic device. A holo-image appeared, showing the meteor shower. "Take this with you," Booster told Superman. "It will help you to find those meteors before they reach the Earth."

Superman took the device. "But what about you and Skeets?" he asked.

"We'll be back home by the time you return," Booster promised. "You know, back where we belong."

Superman shook Booster's hand. "I know you made some mistakes in the past," he said, "but I can see that you're a good person deep down inside."

"Thanks," said Booster Gold. "Coming from you, that means a lot."

ZOOOOOOOOOOOOOOOOOOM!

With that, Superman flew away. The hero needed to stop those meteors before they crashed into Earth!

After Superman was gone, Skeets asked Booster Gold, "What are you planning?"

"What do you mean?" Booster asked, trying too hard to look innocent.

"According to my historical records," Skeet said. "Only one meteor from that meteor shower actually hit the Earth — and it landed harmlessly near a field of cows."

"Harmless?" Booster said with a gasp. "What about the terror those poor cows must have felt? They don't even know what a meteor is! Poor, confused cows."

BEEP BEEP BEEP!

"Booster," Skeets said in a low drone. "I have a built-in lie detector, you know."

Booster frowned. He pointed down at the gathering crowds of people below them. "Let's just stay for the parade," he said. "We'll stay for just a couple more hours, and then we'll go back to the 25th century. That's all. I promise!"

Skeets let out what seemed to be a sigh. "Fine," he said.

* * *

Minutes later, Booster Gold was standing in front of a huge crowd of people. It looked like everyone in Metropolis had come out to celebrate Booster Gold Day.

The mayor had just finished speaking.

Then, Booster Gold stepped up to the podium. "Metropolis!" he called out. "Let's hear it for . . . me!"

With that, the crowd went wild. They cheered and clapped. They shouted, "Booster Gold! Booster Gold! Booster Gold!"

It was the happiest moment of Booster's life.

But just then, Booster Gold felt a horrible shaking beneath his feet.

"Is there supposed to be an earthquake today?" Booster asked Skeets.

"There's no record of it in my database," Skeets answered.

People were panicking as the entire city trembled. A few of the banners fell from the sky and the mayor ran away from the stage.

"We're doomed! We're all horribly doomed!" Booster cried.

"You got that right!" Stompa said. She walked right up to the main stage where Booster Gold was standing. She stuck her thumb out at Booster. "And I'm gonna show this fool what real power looks like!"

Stompa stomped her feet on the ground. *FOOOOOOOOOOOOOM!* Another wave of energy shook the city. People fell to the ground and several of the vending stands shattered with a *CRASH!*

"Where's Superman?" someone cried out. "He'll save us!"

Booster Gold knew that Superman couldn't save anyone. He was in outer space, chasing a meteor shower.

"Let me introduce you to some friends

of mine," Stompa bellowed, interrupting Booster's thoughts. "Rosie and her Demolition Team!"

Rosie appeared, followed by Hardhat, Steamroller, Jackhammer, and Scoopshovel.

SLAM! CRASH! BANG!

They started tearing up everything in their path.

"A bookstore?" Steamroller cried out. "I hate books!"

CRUNCHHHHHHHH! Steamroller drove his steamroller right over the store, flattening it into the ground.

Scoopshovel and Jackhammer were tearing the main stage apart while Hardhat crushed vending stands. Rosie chased the mayor with her rivet gun.

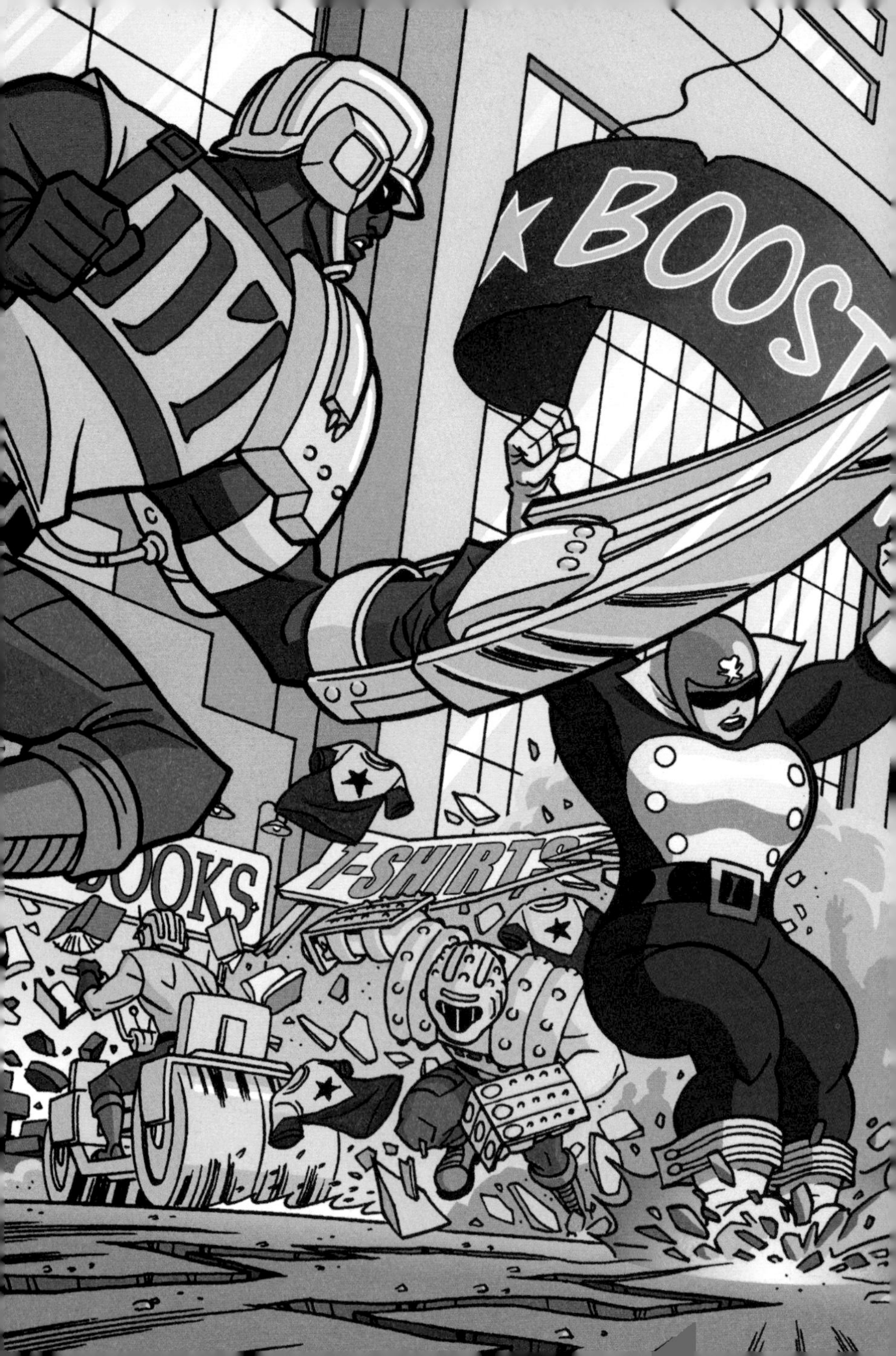

BOOST
BOOKS
T-SHIRTS

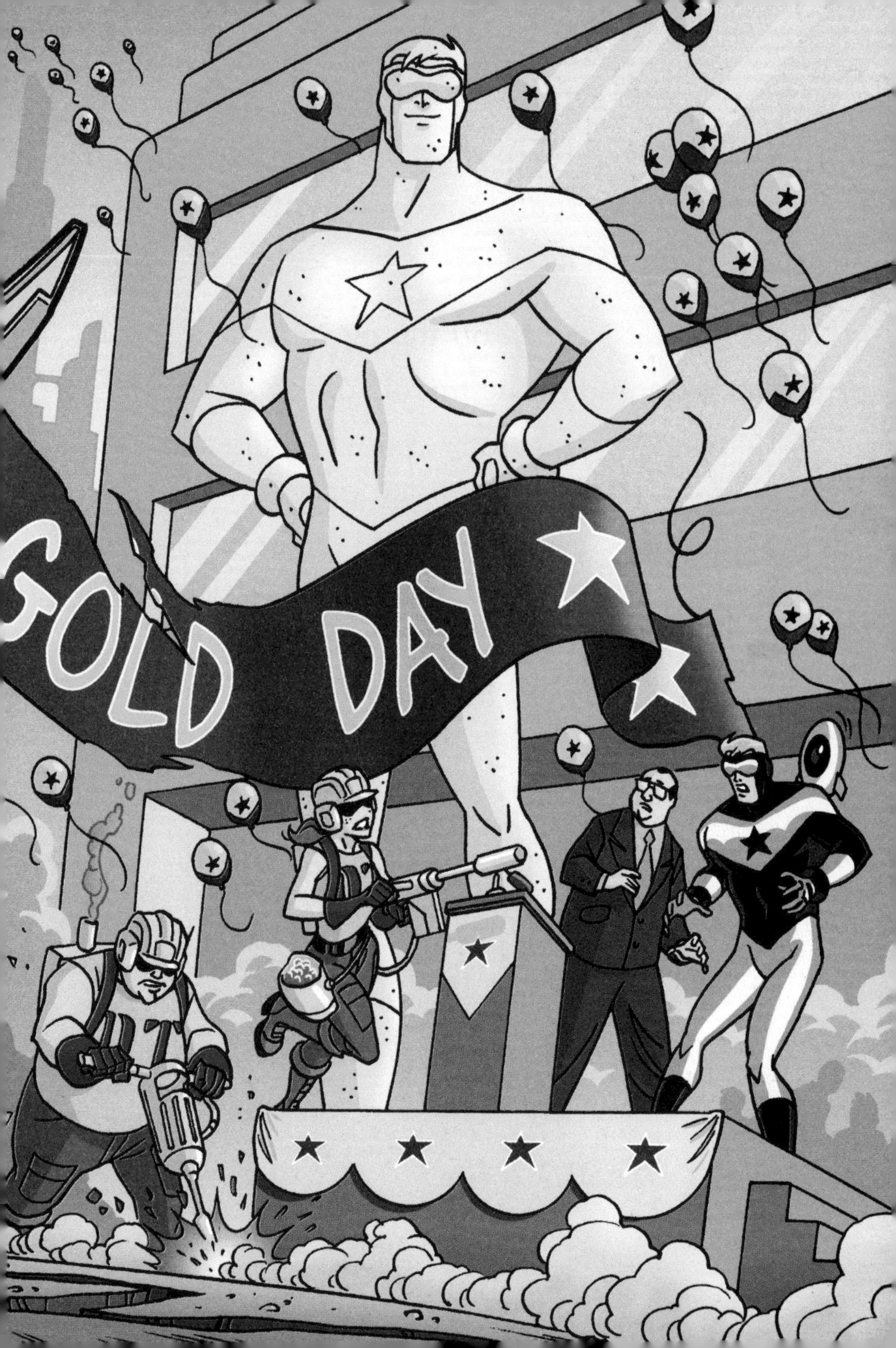
GOLD DAY

"Booster, you need to do something," Skeets said. "You're the only hope these people have!"

Booster jumped off the main stage and was standing in the middle of the street. He was surrounded by chaos. People were screaming and running in all directions. He didn't know where to begin.

Booster's shoulders slumped. "What can I do?" he finally replied. "I'm not a real super hero like Superman. I can't stop a whole team of super-villains!"

Booster watched helplessly as Stompa walked over to the gigantic stature of Booster Gold.

"Here's what I think of this zero!" Stompa shouted.

KA-BOOOOOM!

She stomped her foot next to the statue and sent a wave of energy through it. The statue shook, and then it slowly began to fall over.

Booster watched in horror. "Those people will be crushed!" he told Skeets.

"They will if you don't save them," Skeets agreed. "It's time for you to start acting like a real hero!"

Booster Gold didn't feel like a hero. He was scared. But he couldn't let innocent people suffer because of him. Booster flew up and grabbed the statue by its head, trying to hold it up. "Skeets!" he cried. "Tell me when everyone's gotten out of the way!"

Below, people were running in all directions. They were terrified of Stompa and the Demolition Team.

"Skeets!" Booster cried out. "Can I let go?"

"There are still people directly below you, sir," Skeets answered. "If you let go of that statue, it will land on them!"

Booster's flight ring was powerful, but the statue was simply too heavy. Booster strained, using all of his strength to keep the statue from falling.

"I can't . . . keep this up . . . much longer," he gasped. Booster was doing his best, but now he was stuck underneath the statue, his entire body pressed up against the face of the Booster Gold statue, staring at it eye-to-eye.

"I can't believe . . . the last thing I'm going to see before I die . . . is my own stupid face," Booster said.

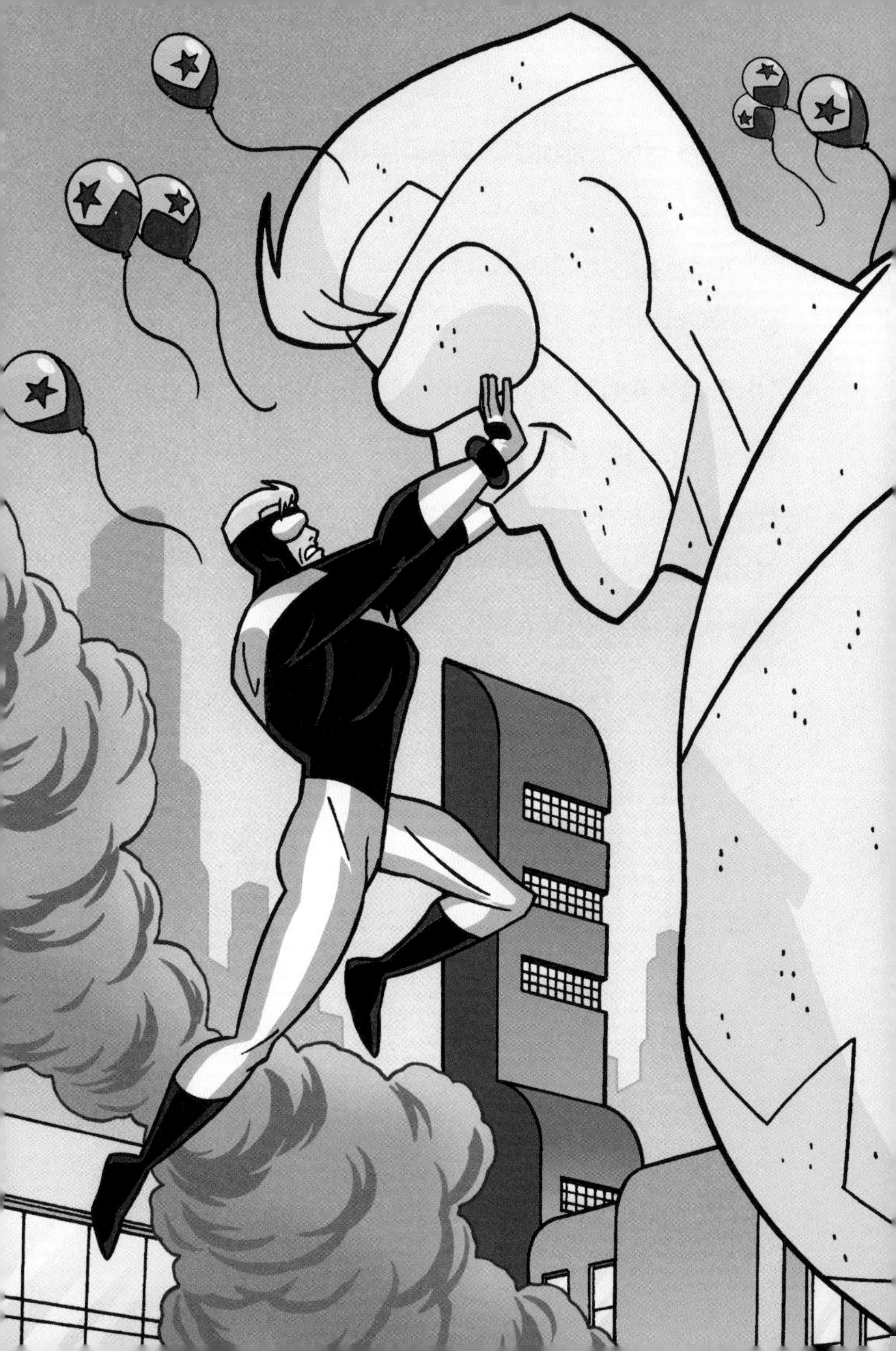

Skeets whizzed through the crowd. "Move out of the way!" he cried out. "You're about to be crushed by Booster's giant ego!"

But even if he managed to clear the area of all people, it was too late for Booster Gold. In just a few moments, the statue would collapse onto the street and Booster Gold would be crushed beneath it.

CHAPTER 5

A REAL HERO

Meanwhile, Superman was busy flying through outer space toward the meteor shower that Booster had said was going to crash into Earth. Superman punched the meteors as they flew toward him, pounding them to dust.

POW!

WHAM!

KRAKABOOOOOOM!!

Just a few more punches and his work would be finished.

BEEP! BEEP! Just then, Superman remembered the Booster Gold Parade. As a reporter, it was his job to write all the big events in Metropolis.

Realizing that he would probably miss the beginning of the event, Superman used his super-vision. Since he couldn't get back to Metropolis right away, he'd watch it from outer space.

ZAPPPPPP!

His vision zoomed in, but Superman didn't see people marching in a parade. Instead, he saw total chaos!

POOF! WOOOOOOOOSH!

Using his super-breath, Superman blew the last few meteors away from Earth. Then he turned around and raced back to Metropolis.

It was a great distance, but innocent lives were at risk, so Superman used his super-speed to fly faster than he'd ever flown before.

FWOOOOOOOOOOOOOOM!

Back in Metropolis, Skeets had cleared out the last few people from beneath the falling statue. "It's okay, sir," Skeets told Booster Gold. "You can let it fall now."

Booster could not even speak. He was using every ounce of his strength to hold up the giant statue. Now, however, he could finally release it. There was no way for him to get out from under the statue, but at least he'd managed to save the citizens of Metropolis.

"If I die," he said to himself, "at least I'll die a hero!"

Just as the statue started to fall, Booster saw a red-and-blue blur take the statue from his hands.

It was the Man of Steel!

"I think this belongs over here," Superman said, placing the statue back on its base. Then he turned to Booster Gold. "So, Booster, are you ready for your very first super hero team-up?"

Booster grinned. "You bet I am!" he said.

Superman and Booster Gold flew, side by side, straight at the Demolition Team.

WHAM!

BAM!!

SLAM!!!

Hardhat, Scoopshovel, and Jackhammer were knocked down like bowling pins.

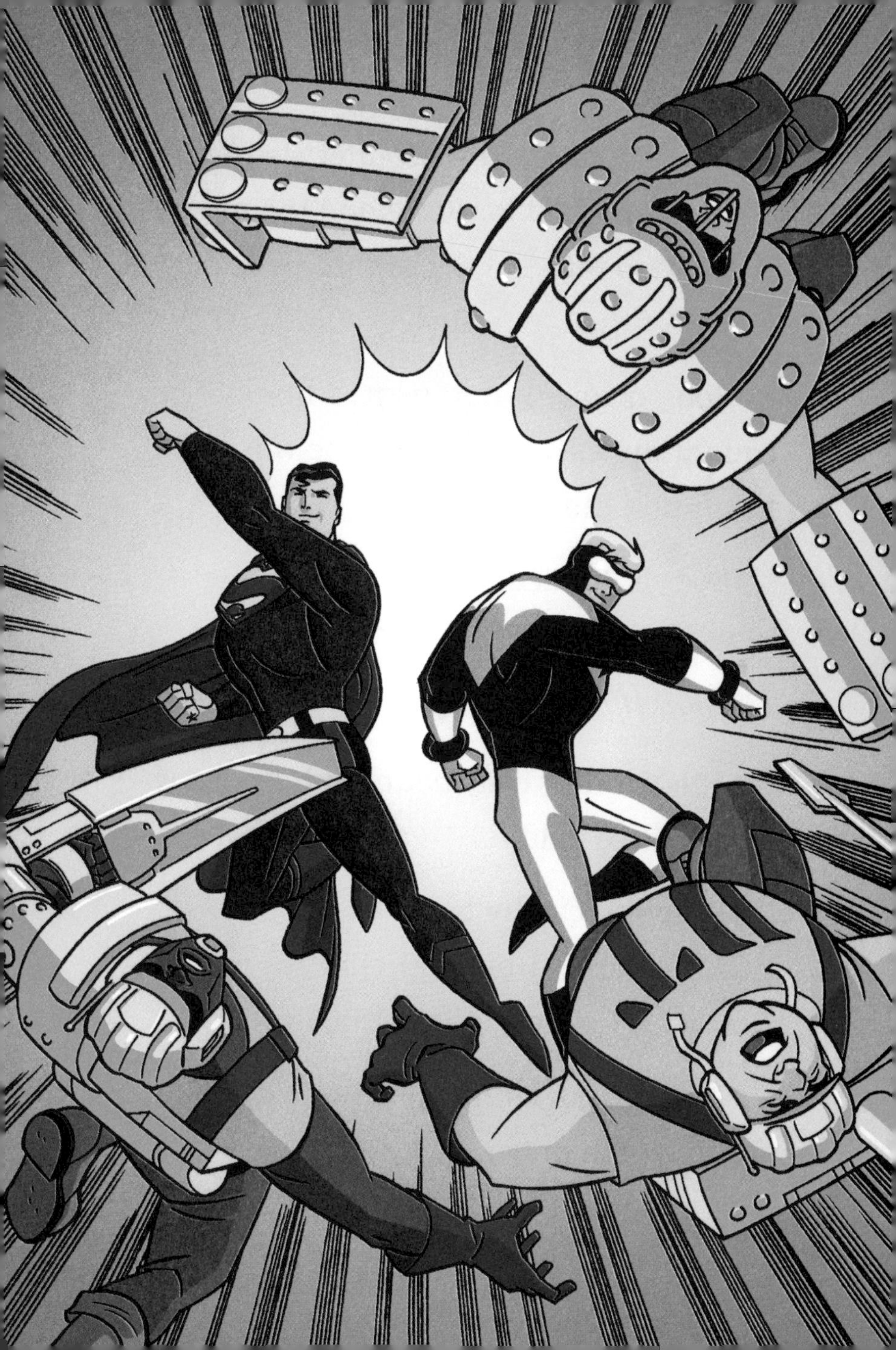

While Superman went after Steamroller, Booster searched for Rosie and the mayor. He flew up into the sky so that he could get a view of the entire city.

Booster saw that Rosie had finally caught up with the mayor. She was about to capture him!

Booster landed right in front of the mayor and stood there, grinning.

TING! TING! TING!

The red-hot rivets bounced harmlessly off his force field.

Followed closely by Skeets, Booster grabbed Rosie. Holding her in his arms, Booster lifted her up into the air.

"Let me go, let me go!" Rosie cried out, fuming with anger.

Booster carried Rosie out over the lake. "Rosie, you need to cool down a bit," he said. And with that, he dropped her into the water.

SPLASH!

"You really need to work on your wit, sir," Skeets observed.

"Don't ruin the moment," Booster said. "I'm teaming up with Superman and fighting a gang of super-villains. Life doesn't get much better than this!"

When Booster returned to the downtown area, he saw that Superman had already captured the rest of the Demolition Team. But while Superman was busy rescuing people from all of the destruction that the villains had caused, Stompa was getting away.

"Do you think you can handle one more super-villain?" Superman asked Booster.

"You bet," Booster said. Then he added, "Partner!"

Superman pointed in the direction that he'd seen Stompa running. "Be careful, though. She's by far the most dangerous of the bunch."

Booster and Skeets raced toward Stompa. They soon saw she had almost reached her armored truck to escape.

"Once she gets inside that truck, you'll never stop her!" Skeets warned.

Booster said nothing. He just flew even faster!

FWOOOOOOOOOOOSH!

"Hey, Stompa!" Booster called out.

Stompa turned around to look, eyes wide. "Oh, it's just you!" she said, letting out a sigh of relief. "I was worried it might be Superman — or some other real super hero!"

Booster kept flying straight toward Stompa.

"Are you stupid?" Stompa asked. "You can't handle me! If you come any closer, I'll stomp you beneath my —"

KA-POOOOWWWWW!

Booster Gold whalloped Stompa right in the jaw. He had activated his force field so that it absorbed most of the impact. Even so, Booster could feel the lasting vibration in his hand.

CLINK! CLANKKKKK!

Stompa fell to the ground, unconscious.

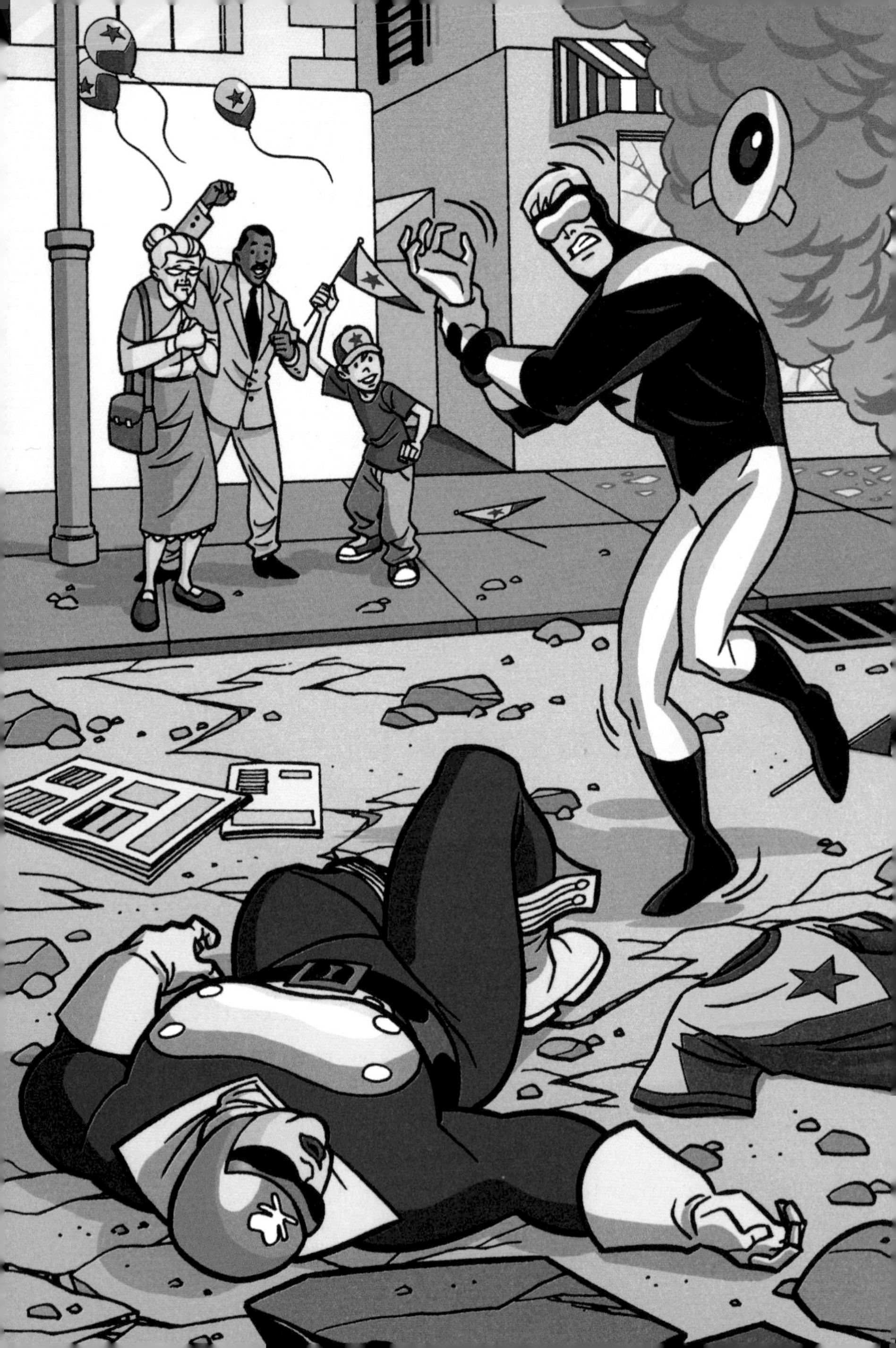

"Wow," Skeets said in admiration. "You knocked her out with one punch!"

Booster Gold landed. At first, he seemed fine. But after a moment, he started clutching his injured hand and jumping up and down. "Ow!" he cried out. "Ow! Ow! Ow! Ow!"

"Are you okay, sir?" Skeets asked.

"It hurts a lot," Booster admitted. "But it was totally worth it!"

*　　*　　*

A few hours later, the sun was just beginning to set. Superman, Booster Gold, and Skeets were gathered on the Daily Planet Building's rooftop. In front of them was an open time-portal that Rip Hunter had provided.

Booster's right hand was wrapped in bandages. His whole body ached. But despite all that . . . he felt great! This had been the best day of his life.

Now, however, it was time to say goodbye to the 21st century. "Can you do me one last favor?" Booster asked Superman.

"What's that?" the Man of Steel asked.

"Please don't tell anyone the truth about me," he pleaded. "Let them think that I was a real super hero. Just this once."

Superman smiled warmly. "You are a real super hero, Booster," he said. "And that's what I'll tell anyone who asks me about Booster Gold."

Booster Gold smiled. "Thanks," he said.

Booster Gold took one final look around and then started to step inside the time portal.

And then he stepped back out again.

"Actually, there is one other thing . . ." Booster said quietly.

Superman rolled his eyes but kept smiling. "Yes, Booster?" he asked. "What do you need?"

"Could you maybe tell everyone that I died saving the universe?" Booster said quickly.

Superman sighed. "I don't think that's a good idea," he said.

Booster continued talking. The more excited he got, the faster the words came out of his mouth.

"You could tell them that someone, maybe some kind of giant, evil space alien was going to blow up the entire planet," Booster babbled, "and then I came swooping in and I shouted, 'I shall not let the Earth be destroyed!' and I sacrificed my life to save the whole, entire universe and then I —"

"Booster —" Superman began to say.

"And you can say that I saved your life!" Booster said. "And Wonder Woman's life, too! I mean, I've never actually met Wonder Woman, but I really don't think she'd mind, she seems like a really nice lady, and —"

"Goodbye, Booster," Superman said with a smirk. Gently, he guided Booster back into the time portal. *ZIPPPPPPPPPP!*

Booster disappeared through the portal, still talking.

As Skeets followed Booster Gold into the time portal, he paused and turned to Superman. "He's really not that bad, you know," Skeets said. "For a human, anyway."

"I know," Superman told Skeets.

*   *   *

The next day, Clark Kent was sitting on the rooftop of the Daily Planet Building. He, Lois, and Jimmy decided to give their outdoor lunch another try.

"So, Booster Gold and Skeets are really gone?" Jimmy asked.

"Yes," Clark said. "Superman said they had to go on an important mission. He doesn't know if we'll ever see them again."

"Well, good riddance!" Lois said, finishing her sandwich. "I honestly don't know how you can defend that Booster Gold. Really, he's no better than Stompa."

"How do you figure that?" asked Jimmy.

"They both just wanted to impress everyone," said Lois. "They were both show-offs."

"Oh, I don't know," said Clark. "Stompa was a bully. She wanted people to fear her. But I think Booster just wanted to feel appreciated. We all need that, sometimes. Maybe even Superman."

"Well," said Jimmy, "I just hope Booster Gold comes back someday. He was kind of a goofball, but it sure was exciting having him around."

"Oh, I have a hunch we haven't see the last of Booster Gold," Clark said, at once happy and nervous over the possibility.

STOMPA

Real Name:
Unknown

Occupation:
Female Fury

Base:
Apokolips

Height:
5 feet, 8 inches

Weight:
330 lbs.

Eyes:
Unknown

Hair:
Unknown

On the alien planet Apokolips — where the super-villain Darkseid rules — Stompa grew up an orphan. At an early age, Stompa's superior strength and ruthlessness drew the attention of Granny Goodness, the orphanage's evil headmistress. Under Granny's strict training and guidance, Stompa became a member of the Female Furies, an elite squad of female warriors. With a determined heart, and a pair of heavy boots, Stompa can't help but make an evil impact.

- Stompa is one of ten members of the Female Furies, an elite group of fighters supporting Darkseid's evil agenda. Other members include Artemis, Mad Harriet, Bernadeth, Bloody Mary, Lashina, Chessure, Malice Vundabarr, Gilotina, and Speed Queen.

- Stompa is the strongest member of the Female Furies. By stomping her oversized boots, the super-villain can create earthquakes large enough to shake and destroy entire cities.

- Durability is another one of Stompa's strengths. Even a superpowered punch from the Man of Steel can't keep this villain down for long

BIOGRAPHIES

PAUL WEISSBURG lives with his wife, Mie, in Rock Island, Illinois, where he teaches political science at Augustana College. Paul read his first comic book in the summer of 1976 and has been an avid comic book reader and writer ever since.

TIM LEVINS is best known for his work on the Eisner Award-winning DC Comics series, Batman: Gotham Adventures. Tim has illustrated other DC titles, such as Justice League Adventures, Batgirl, Metal Men, and Scooby Doo, and has also done work for Marvel Comics and Archie Comics. Tim enjoys life in Midland, Ontario, Canada, with his wife, son, puppy, and two horses.

GLOSSARY

chaos (KAY-oss)—total confusion

concussion (kuhn-KUSH-uhn)—an injury to the brain caused by a heavy blow to the head. A concussion can result in unconsciousness, dizziness, or memory loss.

demolition (dem-uh-LISH-uhn)—destruction or ruin

gimmick (GIM-ick)—a clever gadget, trick, or idea used to get people's attention

massive (MASS-iv)—large, heavy, and solid

pleasant (PLEZ-uhnt)—enjoyable or giving pleasure

ruin (ROO-in)—to spoil or destroy something completely

sacrificed (SAK-ruh-fissed)—gave up something important or enjoyable for a good reason

shattered (SHAT-urd)—broke into tiny pieces

showboating (SHOH-boh-ting)—showing off or trying to attract attention

strained (STRAYND)—drawn or pulled tight, or very tense

DISCUSSION QUESTIONS

1. Would you rather have Booster Gold's superpowers, or Superman's powers? Why?

2. In the end, Booster Gold and Superman make a good team. What makes for a good teammate? Discuss your answers.

3. This book has ten illustrations. Which one is your favorite? Why?

WRITING PROMPTS

1. Do you think Booster Gold is a super hero? What kinds of things does Booster Gold do that are similar to Superman? In what ways are the two men different? Write about it.

2. Imagine you have a talking robot like Skeets for a friend. Write about your robot. What does it do? What does it look like? How does it help you? Write about it, then draw a picture of your robotic pal.

3. Do you think Booster Gold and Superman remain friends after this story ends? Write another chapter to this story where Superman and Booster Gold are reunited. What happens? Write about it!

LOOK FOR MORE

THE MAN OF STEEL™

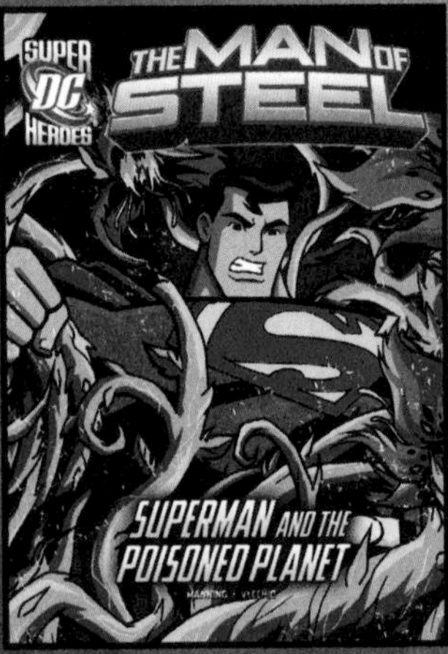
SUPER DC HEROES
THE MAN OF STEEL
SUPERMAN AND THE POISONED PLANET

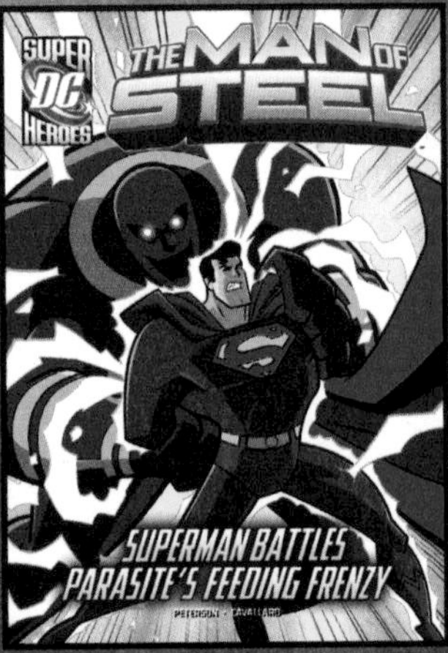
SUPER DC HEROES
THE MAN OF STEEL
SUPERMAN BATTLES PARASITE'S FEEDING FRENZY

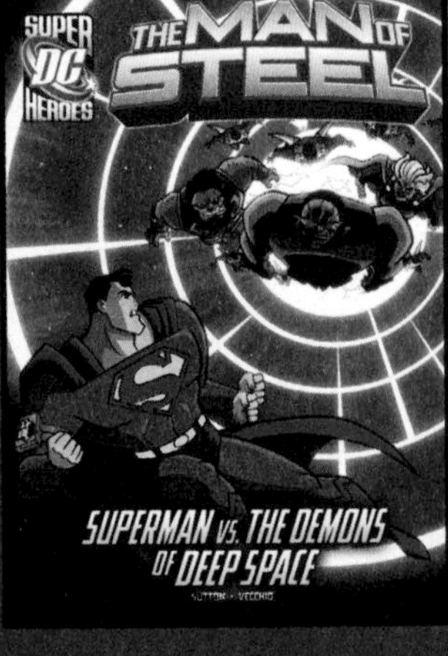
SUPER DC HEROES
THE MAN OF STEEL
SUPERMAN VS. THE DEMONS OF DEEP SPACE

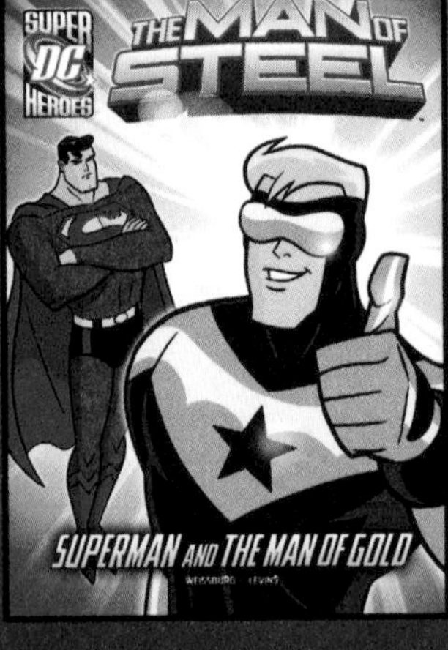
SUPER DC HEROES
THE MAN OF STEEL
SUPERMAN AND THE MAN OF GOLD

THE MAN OF STEEL™

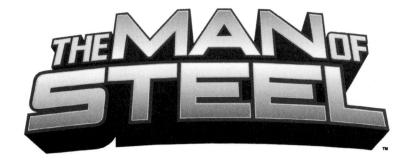